Kathryn B. Grayson-Thomas

He's All I Got

A Fictional Story

He's All I Got

By Kathryn B. Grayson-Thomas

Illustrations by Daniel Henderson

My name is Aniyah Young; I want to tell you a story about a young girl and her two children who struggled through the ups and downs of the drug world. The two children were born into poverty; their lives were like a rollercoaster. Full of highs and lows, seeing nothing but drug addicts, drug use, and all the chaos that came with it. People were sitting and sleeping in empty houses, wherever possible, and so did they. Never knowing where they would end up day-to-day. Their mother would constantly leave them alone, which kept them fearful and wondering if she would return or if something may have happened to her. But she always came back for them. One day, she got a hotel room, which made them feel a little bit safer.

So come on and take this ride with me…

There was a young girl who started life growing up on the east side of Wilmington, DE. Wilmington was a nice place to live compared to other cities. Everyone knew everyone and treated each other like family, and the projects were no different. She was just a teenager when she began hanging out with the wrong crowd, as some teenagers do. Unfortunately, she eventually got caught up in the drug world, became addicted to drugs and was really bad off.

She became uncontrollable and would constantly run away, ignoring her parent's pleading to "straighten up or else." She got pregnant, and her adoptive parents, who had taken all they could of this behavior, reached their limit and threw her out of their home.

3

Now she was on her own and had to survive on the streets the best way she knew how. As time went on, she had another baby. The struggle became real, and things got completely out of control. As sad as it may seem, that's the way things were.

Once drugs become a priority to a person, the things and people that use to matter don't matter anymore. Unfortunately, in this case, the people she could no longer care for or about, the way a mother should, were her two children, Kisha and Jay. She loved them, but she loved her drugs even more. You see, drugs overpower all; since her heart wasn't in the right place when it came to raising her children, it just became too hard for her.

They were too much of a burden because she was just a child herself. Kisha and Jay were left alone to fend for themselves most of the time. They grew very close to each other and became best of friends. They loved each other very much and felt that they were all each other had. Jay stuck to Kisha like glue, as though he would lose the only loved one he had left. You see, their mother was an only child and the children never knew their fathers, never saw their grandparents or any other relatives, for that matter.

Kisha was a cute little 11-year-old girl with long braided hair and pretty brown skin. She was quite thin but tall for her age. She loved to play with her dolls in the dollhouse, and she loves reading her books.

Her mother gave her those books to keep her occupied. Reading kept her mind off the sadness she felt when she and Jay were left alone.

Jay was just a 5-year-old boy with a small round-shaped face and a beautiful smile, which you didn't see much because he was always crying, and he always seemed very timid. He longed for attention and needed to feel the love and warmth from his mommy, but she just wasn't there for them.

Kisha had to console her little brother the best way she knew how which was by reading to him or giving him little toys to play with.

It was so hard and scary for Kisha; there was something about her life that she just didn't understand.

As time when on, the one thing that Kisha always dreaded would happen happened.

They were left alone to fend for themselves once again in the little old dirty hotel room where they were staying when suddenly there was a knock on the door.

Even though Kisha was scared to open the door (which her mom told her never to do), she opened it anyway, and there stood two strangers. Kisha was in complete shock as she stood there with her mouth dropped open. They asked Kisha if her mother was at home as they politely forced their way through the door while glancing around the small room.

Kisha knew this was not good; she felt as if they were in trouble as she looked up at this tall woman standing in her home. Kisha could see the judgment in their faces as they looked around the room and then at her and Jay, noticing their clothes were quite dirty and wrinkled.

The kids looked to not have been bathed for some time, and their hair hadn't been combed in quite a while.

Kisha was hoping and praying her mommy would show up. She thought to herself, *"Please, mommy come home,"* but she didn't.

She even told the lady a little lie when the lady asked where her mother was. She told the lady that her mother went to the store and that she would be right back. But she never came home that day.

That day Kisha and Jay were placed in the foster home of a nice middle-aged couple named Mr. and Mrs. Townsend. The Townsends were good people, but their house was full of all the foster children they had taken in. Most of them came from the same situation as Kisha and Jay.

There must have been at least 13 children in this house. Kisha thought very highly of the Townsends. They gave as much love and attention to the children as possible. Although they didn't get the attention they longed for, some attention was better than what they previously got, which was "nothing."

The Townsends were foster parents and always looking for adoptive parents to come in and adopt out the children. They were getting up in age, and there were children constantly entering the home to be adopted. The drug problem was really getting bad, and so many people were losing their children due to drugs.

Kisha was a very intelligent little girl, but she had to grow up fast because she had to take care of herself as well as her little brother. Kisha was beginning to get use to the house and all the children in it, but it wasn't as easy for Jay.

Everywhere Kisha went, Jay would grab her hand and tag along. Even when she played with other children her own age, he would be right there up under her. She had a hard time getting him to play with the other children his age.

But after a few days of talking to him and assuring him that he would be alright and that she loved him and would always be there for him no matter what. He began to relax and accept the other children, playing games, running, having fun, and playing with the cars and trucks with the other little boys. He actually began to have fun.

They were able to laugh again, something they hadn't done in a long time.

One night while lying in bed, Jay started thinking about his mother.

Jay asked Kisha, "Kisha, where's mommy? When is she coming back? I want my mommy."

"I don't know," Kisha said, "I guess she don't want us, maybe she ain't coming back, I don't know Jay."

"You ain't never gonna leave me, is you?"

"No, ah course not!" said Kisha.

"Why you ask me a stupid question like that, Jay?"

"Ummm, I don't know, I just was thinking bout it, I wanna be sure. Cause you always say you love me like mommy always say she love me, so I just wanna be for sure," replied Jay.

"Nah, I'll never leave you; sisters and brothers are posed to stay together."

"But what about mommy's and daddy's, are they 'pose to stay with their kids too?" asked Jay.

"Yeah, but sometimes I guess they just forget. I don't know, I don't know about the grownups sometimes," said Kisha, with her head lying in the palm of her hand on her pillow.

"They can be crazy people sometimes, or maybe they change their mind, and they don't want kids."

"I want my mommy," said Jay.

"Me too," Kisha whispered; they both began to tear up. Kisha held Jay in her arms, and they cried themselves to sleep.

The next morning, Kisha woke up and looked over at Jay to see him staring her in her eyes.

She popped up and said, "What's wrong with you boy? Why you staring at me like that?"

Jay giggled and said, "Nothing."

"I was waiting for you to wake up."

"Come on," Kisha said, time to go downstairs and eat; the Townsends are waiting probably.

"And I guess some people will be coming to see if there is any of us kids they want to want."

"Not me," said Jay.

So, she and her little brother went to the bathroom to get ready for breakfast.

On the way downstairs, Kisha heard Mrs. Townsends talking to some other adults. She stopped and held her arm out to stop Jay. She listened quietly so she could hear what they were saying.

Mrs. Townsend said, "And he's such a sweet little boy, but I think you'll have a tough time getting him away from his sister, which I don't think can happen. They're very close to each other. I just don't know about those two."

Kisha could not hold back; she jumped down the last three steps, screaming out loud, "Please don't let them take my little brother from me; he's all I got! Please, Mrs. Townsend, please!"

The adults all turned to look with their shocked faces towards Kisha and Jay.

She cried, squeezing her little brothers' hand while holding and tugging at Mrs. Townsend's arm with the other. Jay held on to Kisha as tight as he could, and the tears began to flow down his face as he shook his head, no, no, no.

Mrs. Townsend walked over to the two children and held them close, and said, "Don't worry, kids, no one is going to take you from each other."

The lady looked down at the two and said softly, "I won't take your little brother away from you."

Mrs. Townsend asked the kids to go upstairs and wash their faces.

"Then you can come back down to eat your nice hot breakfast."

For the rest of the day, Jay stuck to Kisha like glue. She could not take a step without him being right there. Just as they began to wind down, another couple came through. Of course, the kids were nervous but soon relieved when they found out they were looking for a newborn, and there happened to be a few babies there. But the sad thing about it was that one of the babies may have contracted AIDS from its drug-addicted mother. It is also sad when someone leaves and you have to say goodbye, knowing that's the last time you'll see them. Seeing this happen did not sit well with Kisha and Jay. Now, everywhere Kisha went, Jay would grab her hand and tag along.

It was about two weeks later when Mr. and Mrs. Townsends' daughter came to visit, and while she was there, she talked to her mother about some problems she was having.

Kisha was in the dining area when she heard Mrs. Townsends' daughter saying, "Mother, the doctor said because, of my past problems, we would never be able to have any kids."

Mrs. Townsends' daughter laid her head on her mother's chest as she began to cry.

"Well, honey, you have to get a second opinion," said Mrs. Townsend.

"That's just it mother, I did, and this doctor feels the same way!"

"What does Bernie think about it?" asked Mrs. Townsend.

"He's just as upset about it as I am," answered her daughter.

Kisha just had to see what Mrs. Townsends' daughter looked like. Because if she looked anything like Mrs. Townsend, she had to be a pretty lady. *"And she was,"* Kisha thought as they looked at each other at the same time, staring into each other's eyes.

At that moment, Kisha thought she was just the most beautiful woman she had ever seen. She had pretty dark smooth skin, her eyes were beautiful and big, and she had a big, beautiful smile with pearly white teeth. Kisha's eyes just locked on her as she spoke to her.

"Hi, little girl," she said, smiling through her tears, looking right into Kisha's eyes.

"*She is so pretty*," Kisha thought as she looked back into her eyes.

She barely got it out, but she did manage to say hi back to the lady. And then her mind started to wander, and her wishing kicked in. "*I wonder what kind of mommy she would be like. I wonder if she's a nice person. What's her husband like? Would she take my brother and me? Would Jay like 'em? I wish she was Jay's and my mother.*"

"You're a very pretty little girl; what's your name?" asked the lady.

"Thank you, my name is Kisha, and you're very pretty too."

The lady smiled just as Mrs. Townsend spoke up and said, "Kisha, this is my daughter Anndria."

"Oh," said Kisha, "I didn't know you had your own kids, Mrs. Townsend."

"Yes," said Mrs. Townsend.

"I have two sons and a daughter. Yup, I raised three beautiful children of my own before I took on this second responsibility of taking care of all of you. I guess I just love children," she said, smiling as she reached out to take her daughter's hand.

And now, her own daughter was dealing with the problem of not being able to bear her own children. That made Kisha feel kind of sad. Kisha felt confused about all the problems that people must face in this world. Then she realized she and her brother were not the only ones facing such hard problems.

She thought to herself, *"The world must be a tough place to live in."*

At that moment is when she realized, *"I'm going to beat this world and its problems. Me and my brother, we're going to do it together."*

Just as she started to turn and walk away, she heard Miss Anndria say, "Bye-bye."

"Bye-bye," replied Kisha as she and Jay went on their way.

Kisha could hear Mrs. Townsend telling her daughter about her little brother as they walked away. Her daughter was there for a good part of the day before she left. When she was ready to leave, she made sure to say goodbye to Kisha and Jay, specifically calling them by their names. Kisha thought that was so nice of her. It made her feel really special. She and Jay watched her as she drove off, waving with great big smiles until the car was out of sight.

That night as they lay in bed, Kisha told Jay about Miss Anndria's problems and how she couldn't have children.

"Jay," said Kisha.

"Huh," replied Jay.

"Do you think you would like Miss Anndria as a mother?"

"I don't know," said Jay, "is she nice?"

"I think so. With parents like Mr. and Mrs. Townsend, she must be," replied Kisha.

"Don't she have her own kids and boyfriend? Dey might not want no more kids."

"No, she don't have kids," said Kisha, "and she can't have none. But don't say nothing bout that. I heard her tell her mom that. So, she is going to maybe pick somebody from here. And maybe it could be us. Uh-huh, that sure would be nice. And she's pretty too, you think?"

"I guess," said Jay, "whatta bout her boyfriend?"

"She don't have a boyfriend," said Kisha, "he's her husband."

"What's a husband?" asked Jay.

"A husband is when a man and lady get married," said Kisha.

"Married?" asked Jay.

"Oh My God Jay!" said Kisha, "I'll tell you about that some other day. Anyways she seems nice, so she must have a nice husband. She's just got to."

"Whatta bout mommy?" asked Jay.

"I don't know about mommy or where she is. She don't want us anyway!" she said angrily.

Soon the two fell asleep. Kisha had the most beautiful dream that night about Miss Anndria adopting her and Jay.

It took a little time, but Kisha and Jay were getting used to living in the big house with all the other children. They were beginning to feel like family, and Jay started to loosen up and play with the other little boys. Kisha would watch him and smile, seeing him laughing and having fun made her feel really good. This allowed Kisha to play with the bigger kids and enjoy playing with dolls, talking with the other girls, and giggling as little girls do. It took a lot of the bad thoughts off her mind, and she began to relax and feel at home.

Three weeks had gone by when Kisha's dreams were almost crushed. A couple stopped over to look at the children while the children were in the yard playing. Kisha could see Mrs. Townsend pointing out kids and telling the folks about them one by one. Kisha just knew Mrs. Townsend would not let her down by separating her and her brother because they just could not be separated. But for some reason, when that lady saw Kisha, she wanted her as her child. As they walked towards Kisha, she began to get scared. Jay grabbed Kisha's hand and began to squeeze it very tightly.

Mrs. Townsend approached Kisha and looked down at her with very sad eyes and said, "Kisha, this is Mrs. Johnson, she's looking for one child, and that's a little girl. And she thinks you might be the perfect one."

"You mean she wants my little brother and me, right?" asked Kisha.

"No, she's only looking for one child, and that's a little girl. And she thinks you might be the one."

"But Mrs. Townsend, you know I can't go without my little brother. You know I can't leave Jay. Please, Mrs. Townsend! Please don't let her take me from my brother! I won't go! I won't go!" she pleaded as Jay began to cry.

Mr. Townsend looked at Jay and said, "Son, don't cry; you have to be happy for your sister. Somebody is ready to take her and make a good home for her."

"But this is a good home right here," Jay cried.

"We can't keep you here forever," said Mrs. Townsend.

"I know," said Kisha, "but just 'til the right people come along."

"But Kisha, who knows when that will be. And the Johnson's are nice people, but they only want one child."

Mr. Johnson stooped down and held Kisha's hand and said, "Kisha, you'll be very happy in our home if you just give us a try."

Kisha cried, "I don't want to give it a try. I don't want to leave my brother. Not for you, not for anybody!"

The adults kept trying to reason with Kisha and Jay. Mr. Townsend then said, "Kisha, there are so many kids that need a place to stay, and they have nowhere to go. You have been blessed with that chance, and you can't pass it up. And then there will be room for another child to come and stay here. You understand that, don't you?"

"NO! Take somebody else," Kisha cried.

Jay grabbed Kisha, crying, "Don't leave me, Kisha, don't let them take you away from me!"

Kisha walked over to Mrs. Johnson, and she looked at her with great big-ole tears in her eyes and said, "Please, Ma'am, He's All I Got; he's all the family I got in this whole wide world. If you take me, I won't have nobody; please don't take me from my brother."

Soon they ran out of things to say to the children and began to get frustrated with them; Mr. Townsends' voice was starting to get loud, "Kisha!" he said sternly, and then his daughter walked in.

Kisha ran to her and grabbed her and cried, "don't let 'em take me, Miss Anndria, don't let them take me from my brother, please," as she sniffled really hard.

Just then, Anndria's husband Bernie walked in; he was there to meet and see the children. Anndria had been excitedly telling him about a brother and sister that she met at her mother's house. Mrs. Townsend started to introduce everyone.

"Mother," Anndria said, "Bernie and I had a long discussion, and we've decided that we want to adopt. And we want to adopt from right here."

Mrs. Townsends' eyes brightened up and she was lost for words.

"Really?" she asked her daughter, "you're really going to adopt? That's wonderful; that's just a lovely thing to do. I can't believe it. So many children need parents who can give them love these days."

She grabbed her daughter and hugged her, and then hugged her son-in-law. She was so overjoyed she hugged everyone standing around.

"Well, look around," said Mr. Townsend.

"We don't have to," said Anndria, "we know exactly who we want."

She and her husband Bernie both turned around and looked at Kisha and Jay. Kisha and Jay couldn't believe what they were hearing. They both jumped and ran to Mr. and Mrs. Parker at the same time. They ran right into their new parent's arms. Mr. Parker picked Jay up and gave him a great big hug, and Jay hugged him back as tightly as he could. It felt so good to be held by a dad and to know that he would have a daddy now. They hadn't felt so happy in such a long time, or maybe never. They just couldn't stop hugging their new parents.

The Townsends looked at the Johnson's and said, "Well, if you'd like to look around some more, you are more than welcome. I'm sure you can find another nice little girl you could take home and call your own."

Jay lifted his head off his new daddy's shoulder and said, "Cause it ain't gonna be my Kisha."

Everyone laughed; they were all happy for Jay and Kisha, even the Johnson's. So, they began checking out the other children.

In the meantime, Kisha and Jay were happily meeting their new parents and grandparents. The look of relief was in Kisha and Jay's faces, and their smiles were big, bright and beautiful.

They felt so happy to be together, and they knew it would stay this way. And Kisha knew that this was the beginning of her overcoming the problems of this world. She knew she would make it, and so would Jay.

The End

To every reader of this book, Always Put "GOD" First!

I acknowledge my mother, Evangelist Annie Mae Grayson (whom I loved dearly). My father, Ernest Grayson, father and mother-in-law the late Bunion J. and Sadie Mae Thomas, my husband Keith Thomas Sr., son Keith Jr., daughter Anndria M. Thomas, my step-daughter Latoya Thomas, my beautiful grandchildren Aniyah, Azana, and Jasmyne Thomas, and Jordan Haynes, great-grandchildren Za'niyrah Thomas and Milan Haynes, my Godson Kevin Rasin, Goddaughter Dania Grayson.

To my sister Velma L. Young, brothers Walter, Raymond, Leroy, Larry, and Kevin Grayson.

To the greatest Auntie ever, Bertha L. Parker, my cousin/sister Zelma Blackson.

To my siblings who have passed on sisters Ernestine Johnson, Bertha L. Lingham, and Willie Mae Grayson, my brothers William, Clyde and Bernard Grayson.

To Miss Dorothy Lanier (a devoted friend)

To all my nieces, nephews, cousins, in-laws, and friends.

I Love You All

Thank you so much for your support!

He's All I Got

By Kathryn B. Grayson-Thomas

Illustrations by Daniel Henderson

Editor: Anelda Attaway

Co-editor: Leroy Grayson

Published by Jazzy Kitty Publications, Wilmington, DE 19805

877.782.5550 - http://www.jazzykittypublications.com

Copyright © 2022 Kathryn B. Grayson-Thomas

ISBN 978-1-954425-45-3

Library of Congress Control Number: 2022904202

Credits: Book Cover, image and illustrations by Daniel Henderson; Book Editing by Anelda Attaway Co-editor Leroy Grayson; Logo Designs by Andre M. Saunders and Jess Zimmerman.